For Maurita, Loren, Seth, Emma,
Patrick, and Jackson,
who brightened Elm Place every day
—Charlotte

To my wife, Florence,
for all those missed days at the beach
—W.M.

Charlotte Zolotow

THE SEASHORE BOOK

Paintings by Wendell Minor

HarperCollins*Publishers*

"What is the seashore like?" a little boy asked his mother.

He lived in the mountains and had never seen the sea.

His mother smiled. "Let's pretend," she said.

"It is early morning at the seashore and it's hard to tell where the sea stops and the sky begins.

"They are the same smoky gray until
the mist shifts from gray to dark white,
from dark white to pale purple,
from pale purple to hazy blue,
and then, suddenly,

the sun breaks through!

"It warms the cool sand.
It turns the sea green,
and the beach is golden gray.
You run down to the water's edge,
one small dark spot
against the brightness of the sand and sea.

"You bend over and pick up a stone
washed smooth by the sea.
You find tiny brown snail shells,
and oyster shells, crusty gray outside
and smooth, pearly pink inside.

"You pick up a clam shell half open,
and inside, a live clam
snaps the shell closed."
"In my hand?" the little boy asks.
"In your hand," the mother says.

"Then you reach down again
and pick up a wet white gull feather
from the gulls flying overhead.

"We sit at the edge of the water
and build a castle of wet sand
until the waves wash up and suck it back to sea.
The cold water makes your skin
feel like peppermint,
and you are tired.

"You lie down in the hot noonday sun now,

and it feels warm as a big soft cat

covering you,

taking away the chill of the waves.

The swishswashing sound of them

lulls you to sleep.

"I watch while you sleep,

and you don't see two little gray sandpipers

run past you.

But when you wake up,

you do see their claw prints

like pencil lines in the sand.

"You rub your eyes

and it seems there is nothing in the world

except the sound of the wind

and the rising and falling song of the waves.

"You stand and look at the ocean.
Far, far out, so far it seems a toy,
a little white sailboat skims over the water
and disappears.

"The tide is going out.
'I'm hungry,' you say.
I am too, so we wade over to a big rock
covered with seaweed and moss.
We sit there together and eat our sandwiches
and drink lemonade from our thermos
and watch the small brown sand crabs
squaggling at our toes.

"An airplane flies low in the sky.
Its shadow on the sand is like a gigantic bird,
and you leap off the rock and chase after it
until it is gone.

"I watch you throw your head back
and twirl yourself around and around
until you are too dizzy to stand
and you fall down on the sand.

"The wind is getting cooler.
Long purple streaks of clouds
are forming in the sky.
We take each other's hands
and walk down the beach
toward home.

"The fishing pier we pass
is white as a snowfall
with hundreds of crying sea gulls
waiting for the fishing boats
to come in when the sun sets.

"The evening air is so still
that the life buoy's

DING, DING, DONG

sounds right next to us, close and
clear and loud.

"We climb to the top of the dune,
away from the ocean,
but we stop and look down across the sea grass
to the sea.
The setting sun is a huge orange ball.

"You are so tired when we get home
that you can hardly stay awake
through your hot bath and your dinner.

"We barely have time to kiss good night
before you fall asleep.

"Outside, the lighthouse is flashing
golden gleam on,
golden gleam gone.
But you don't see it;
you are sleeping so deeply.

"You don't hear the tide rising.
You don't see the small crescent moon
outside your window.
The ocean is bursting in waves along the shore,
covering the rock where we sat and ate
our lunch,
and carrying up seaweed and shells
to the sand."

The little boy leaned against his mother
and smiled.

"I like the seashore a lot," he said,

"and now I can always close my eyes
and be there
the way I was just now

with you."

CHARLOTTE ZOLOTOW, as author, editor-publisher, and educator, has one of the most distinguished reputations in the field of children's literature. She has written over sixty well-loved books for young readers, many of which—MR. RABBIT AND THE LOVELY PRESENT and WILLIAM'S DOLL, for example—have become true picture-book classics.

WENDELL MINOR was born in Aurora, Illinois, and was graduated from the Ringling School of Art and Design in Sarasota, Florida. He is the recipient of over two hundred professional awards. He has also illustrated three children's books by Diane Siebert: SIERRA, HEARTLAND, and MOJAVE. Mr. Minor has spent many years painting at the seashore on location at the Outer Banks, North Carolina; Martha's Vineyard, Massachusetts; and Monhegan Island, Maine.

The Seashore Book   Text copyright © 1992 by Charlotte Zolotow   Illustrations copyright © 1992 by Wendell Minor   Printed in the U.S.A. All rights reserved.   1 2 3 4 5 6 7 8 9 10   First Edition   Library of Congress Cataloging-in-Publication Data   Zolotow, Charlotte, date   The seashore book / Charlotte Zolotow ; paintings by Wendell Minor.   p.   cm.   Summary: A mother's words help a little boy imagine the sights and sounds of the seashore, even though he's never seen the ocean.   ISBN 0-06-020213-0. — ISBN 0-06-020214-9 (lib. bdg.)   [1. Seashore—Fiction.   2. Imagination—Fiction.   3. Mothers and sons—Fiction.]   I. Minor, Wendell, ill.   II. Title.   PZ7.Z77Se   1992   [E]—dc20   91-22783   CIP   AC   The illustrations in this book were painted with gouache and watercolors on cold-press watercolor board.